What's In a Tail?

Based on the teleplay by Susan Kim

Adapted by Laura F. Marsh

NATIONAL GEOGRAPHIC
WASHINGTON, D.C.

For Markus and Hannes
— L.F.M.

Book design by Bea Jackson

Photo credits
p 11 (whale tail): Shutterstock; p 12 (sea horses): Ovidiu Iordachi/Shutterstock; p 13 (spider monkey): iStockphoto.com;
p 14 (deer): Nicholas Piccillo/Shutterstock; p 15 (wolves): iStockphoto.com; p 18-19 (baby elephant): Anke van Wyk/Shutterstock

 NATIONAL GEOGRAPHIC

 Founded in 1888, the National Geographic Society is one of the largest nonprofit scientific and educational organizations in the world. It reaches more than 285 million people worldwide each month through its official journal, NATIONAL GEOGRAPHIC, and its four other magazines; the National Geographic Channel; television documentaries; radio programs; films; books; videos and DVDs; maps; and interactive media. National Geographic has funded more than 8,000 scientific research projects and supports an education program combating geographic illiteracy.

For more information, please call
1-800-NGS LINE (647-5463) or write to the following address:
NATIONAL GEOGRAPHIC SOCIETY
1145 17th Street N.W., Washington, D.C. 20036-4688 U.S.A.

Visit us online at www.nationalgeographic.com/books
Librarians and teachers, visit us at www.ngchildrensbooks.org
Visit Mama Mirabelle online at http://littlekids.nationalgeographic.com/littlekids/mamamirabelle/

For information about special discounts for bulk purchases, please contact National Geographic Books Special Sales: ngspecsales@ngs.org.

For rights or permissions inquiries, please contact National Geographic Books Subsidary Rights: ngbookrights@ngs.org.

Library of Congress Cataloging-in-Publication Data available from the publisher on request.
Trade Paperback ISBN 978-1-4263-0430-9
Reinforced Library Edition ISBN 978-1-4263-0431-6

Printed in the United States of America

Max the elephant and Mama Mirabelle found Bo the cheetah and Karla the zebra playing near the acacia tree.

"We're trying to decide who has the coolest tail," said Karla.

"My tail flies out behind me, all spotty and aerodynamic!" Bo said.

"Mine's long and flippy, and stripey," said Karla proudly.
"Those are great tails," Mama Mirabelle agreed.

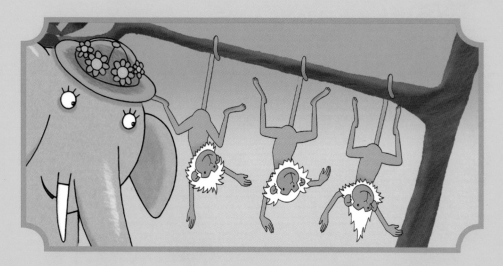

The three monkeys, Flip, Chip, and Kip, swung on a branch upside down.

"Wow! Their tails can hold on to stuff," said Max. He looked sadly back at his own tail.

"Tails do interesting things," said Mama, "and that's something to celebrate. Let's give our tails a shake!"
Everyone was dancing and shaking . . . except Max.

"What can your tail do, Max?" asked Karla.

"Well, uh . . .my tail is sort of gray, and shortish . . ." he replied. "And it has hair on the end."

"Does it grab things?" Bo asked.

"Not really," Max admitted.

Max hung his head and walked slowly away.

Later that day, Mama found him among some large trees. "Maxie, why are you hiding?" she asked kindly.

"Everyone else has a great tail, but mine just sits there," he said.

"Every tail is unique and great," replied Mama. "I have a movie I want you and your friends to see."

"It's **Movie** Time!"

"Some animals use their tails to swim through the water," said Mama. "Wally the whale has a big tail that can take him thousands of miles."

"Wow, that's a long way," Bo said.

"Sea horses can grab onto plants with their tails," said Mama.

"They're my favorite!" Karla exclaimed.

"And spider monkeys use their tails to play and move from tree to tree," said Mama.

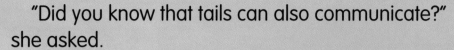

"Did you know that tails can also communicate?" she asked.

"Tails talk?" Karla said.

"Not really. But tails say what animals are feeling," explained Mama. "When the white-tailed deer swishes its tail, other deer know to look out for danger."

"That tail is shaggy," said Bo.

"Wolves wag their tails to tell other wolves they're friendly," Mama said. "And here's another fantastic tail . . ."

"Stop!" Max called out. "These movies aren't making me feel better."

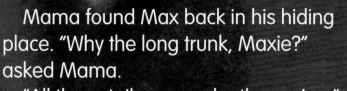

Mama found Max back in his hiding place. "Why the long trunk, Maxie?" asked Mama.

"All those tails are cooler than mine," he answered.

"Remember that each tail is terrific in its own way?" Mama said. Max didn't budge. "Well, the best part is coming up. Will you join us?"

"Okay," Max agreed reluctantly.

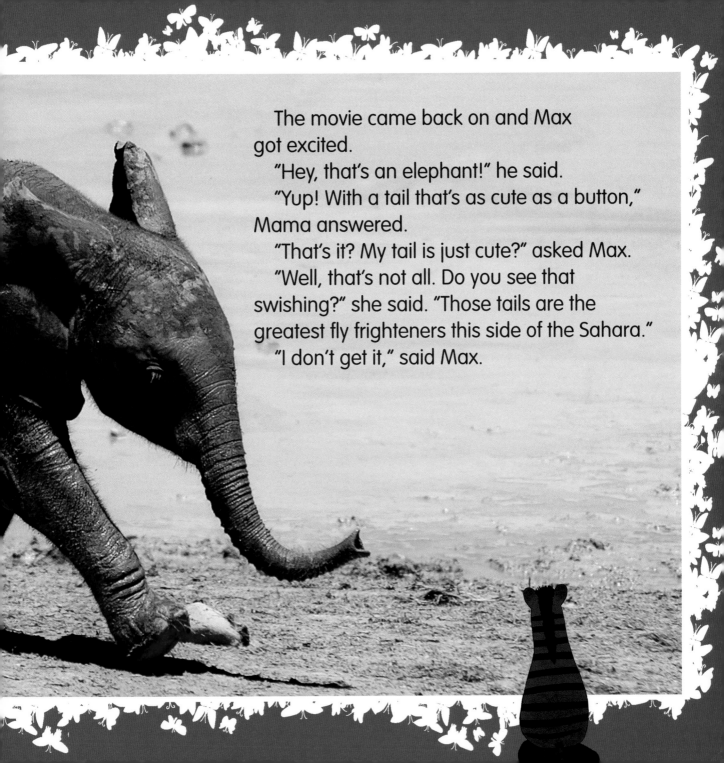

The movie came back on and Max got excited.

"Hey, that's an elephant!" he said.

"Yup! With a tail that's as cute as a button," Mama answered.

"That's it? My tail is just cute?" asked Max.

"Well, that's not all. Do you see that swishing?" she said. "Those tails are the greatest fly frighteners this side of the Sahara."

"I don't get it," said Max.

"Your tail gets rid of bugs, Maxie!" replied Mama. "We don't want pesky biting bugs fluttering around our backsides, do we?"

"No, we don't!" Max said firmly.

"Put it to the test, Max!" said Mama.

A fly came very close to Max's tail. With a big SWISH, he swatted the fly away.

"Wowie Kazowie! Did you see that?" Max asked excitedly.

"That bug won't be coming back here!" said Bo.

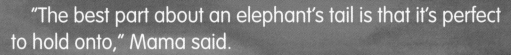

"The best part about an elephant's tail is that it's perfect to hold onto," Mama said.

Then Mama Mirabelle had a great idea.

"Hey, everybody!" she called out. "Get on our conga line and shake that tail!"

Max proudly got behind Mama and grabbed on. The other animals joined in, too.

"Max, do you know my very favorite thing about your tail?"
Mama Mirabelle asked.

"No, tell me," said Max.

Mama smiled at her little elephant. "It's attached to you,"
she said.